CW00847400

*For Louise*

First published in 1991 by
Spindlewood
70 Lynhurst Avenue
Barnstaple
Devon EX31 2HY



Photoset in Galliard
at Five Seasons Press, Hereford

Printed in Great Britain by
Alden Press Ltd, Oxford

British Library Cataloguing in Publication Data

Grandad's new-old nursery rhymes
1. Nursery rhymes
I. Jones, Merlin II. Peters, Margaret
398.8

ISBN 0–907349–62–5 (hardback)
0–907349–82–X (paperback)

# GRANDAD'S NEW-OLD NURSERY RHYMES

Merlin Jones

*Illustrated by Margaret Peters*

“Tell me some nursery rhymes, Grandad,” said Louise, climbing up on to his knee.

“Which do you like best?” asked Grandad. “Old ones or new ones?”

“The old ones, please.”

“Right, let me think now . . . . . . How about these?

I had a little pony once,
His name was Dapple Grey,
I lent him to a lady
To ride a mile away.
She whipped him and slashed him
And rode him through the mire —
I would not lend my horse again
For any lady’s hire.

Wee Willy Winkie runs through the town
Upstairs and downstairs, in his nightgown,
Rapping at the window, crying at the lock,
'Are the children all in bed?
It's past eight o'clock!'

Humpty-Dumpty sat on a wall,
Humpty-Dumpty had a great fall,
And all the King's horses
And all the King's men
Couldn't put Humpty together again!

There was an old woman who lived in a shoe,
She had so many children she didn't know what to do,
So she gave them all broth without any bread,
And whipped them all soundly and sent them to bed.

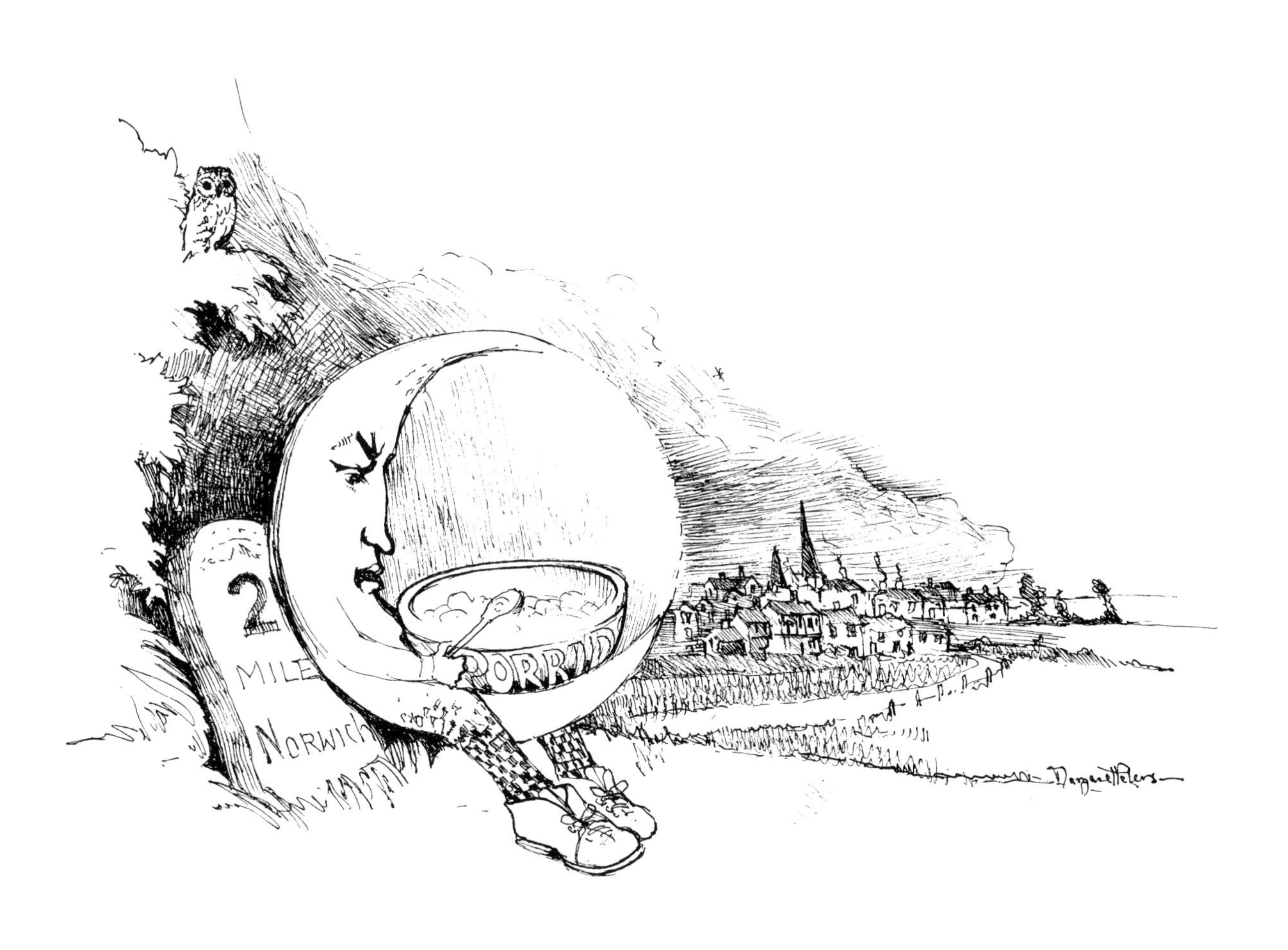


The Man in the Moon came down too soon
And asked the way to Norwich,
He turned to the South and burned his mouth
Through eating cold pease porridge."

"I liked them," said Louise.

"Yes," said Grandpa. "But, you know, I like new-old ones."

"How can they be new *and* old?" said Louise, who was a very sensible little girl.

"I'll tell you one, and then you'll see."

He began,

> "I had a little pony once,
> His name was Dapple . . . Black . . ."

"No, no, Grandad, *Grey*, Dapple *Grey*," said Louise firmly.

"Ah," said Grandad, "but that's the *old* rhyme. As I told you, mine is a *new*-old rhyme."

"I see," said Louise, "go on, then."

Grandad started again,

> "I had a little pony once,
> His name was Dapple Black,
> I lent him to a lady
> And she wouldn't give him back,
> She whipped him and slashed him
> And rode him through the muck —
> I never knew a pony have such rotten luck!"

Grandad was smiling, but Louise looked at him gravely, thinking over his new-old rhyme.

"I still feel sorry for the pony," she said, and Grandad gave her a quick hug.

Louise got down from his knee and went off to play until bed-time.

"Time to go to sleep now," said Louise's mother, tucking her in.

"Oh, Mummy, ask Grandad to come up and tell me another rhyme."

"All right, but only one, mind."

Grandad sat on the edge of the bed, and Louise held his hand.

"Do you know another new-old one?" she asked.

"Well, as it's bed-time, how about Wee Willie Winkie?"

"Does he want to make sure that the children all go to bed by eight o'clock? I don't think much of that!"

"Not in my rhyme, he doesn't; he makes them all get up."

"How does he do that?"

Grandad started, "Wee Willie Winkie runs through the . . ."

He stopped.

"Town?" suggested Louise.

"No," said Grandad, "street, in my rhyme . . .

Wee Willie Winkie runs through the street,
In his old dressing-gown, slippers on his feet,
Rapping at the window, crying in a roar,
'Unless you all get up at once,
I'm breaking down the door!'"

Louise laughed.
"That must have shifted them!" she said.

One day Louise and Grandad were taking a walk through the park when they came to a high fence.

"That reminds me," said Grandad.

"Of what?" said Louise.

"Why, Humpty-Dumpty."

"But that's not a wall, Grandad; Humpty-Dumpty sat on a wall."

"I don't think he was very bright," said Grandad, "so in my book it's

> Humpty-Dumpty sat on a fence,
> Humpty-Dumpty hadn't much sense;
> —It's no good asking for help from a horse,
> He should have gone to a doctor, of course."

"He couldn't do that when he was smashed to pieces," said Louise, who as we know was a very practical girl. "What he needed was a huge tube of glue."

"Quite right," said Grandad; "in that case how about

> Humpty-Dumpty sat on a fence,
> Humpty-Dumpty hadn't much sense;
> If only he'd known the right thing to do
> He'd have carried around a huge tube of glue."

Louise clapped her hands in delight.
"That would have done it!" she said.

They walked on until they came to a park bench, where they sat down and shared a bag of crisps.

While they were munching Grandad said, "What about that old woman who lived in a shoe? Very odd, that; I've always thought that it must have been an extremely tight squeeze. Ought to have been a boot, at the very least. And I didn't much care for the way she gave them no bread, and whipped them all soundly and sent them to bed."

"Nor me," said Louise. "Can we do better with a new-old rhyme?"

Grandad started,

> "There was an old woman who lived in a boot."

Louise added,

> "She fed all her children on chocolates and fruit."

Grandad finished,

> "And when that was gone, to feed their poor faces
> They all climbed out and ate the boot laces!"

"Ugh," said Louise, "they must have tasted awful!"

"Not at all," said Grandad, "you see, they were liquorice laces."

At tea-time, after she had eaten her bread-and-butter, Louise reached out her hand for one of the cakes, which all had different coloured icing on top. She couldn't make up her mind which one to pick, but finally selected the pink one.

"That reminds me," said Grandad.

"Oh dear," said Louise. "Here we go again. I suppose it's another new-old one?"

"You're right," he said, and began, "I had a little pony once . . ."
"But we've had that one, Grandad."
"Oh no," he said, "this is quite different:

I had a little pony once,
His name was Dapple Pink,
I took him to the water
But couldn't make him drink,
I pushed him and pulled him,
And got in quite a state;
I never knew a pony
Be so obstinate!"

Louise smiled. "I like that," she said. "That little pony is showing some spirit at last. I wonder what he'll do next?"
"Wait and see," said Grandad.

---

Next day when Louise came home from school Grandad asked her what she had learned.

She said, "We had a lesson about astronauts going up into space in rockets. Two of them landed on the Moon, and others went round and round the Earth."

"I know," said Grandad, who knew *everything*. "Once round the Earth is called a circuit. The Man-in-the-Moon in the nursery rhyme — he must have been an astronaut, don't you think?"

"I suppose so," said Louise doubtfully, "but that was a long time ago, before space travel was invented."

"Oh, I think he was," said Grandad, "but he couldn't have been a very good one if he came down too soon and had to ask the way to Norwich. And then he went and burned his mouth through eating cold pease porridge, silly fellow."

"I don't see how he could burn himself with cold pease porridge," said Louise.

"Well," said Grandad, "perhaps up on the Moon cold is hot and hot is cold, and he'd got used to things being like that."

"Anyway," said Louise, "it doesn't make much sense, so let's do a new-old one."

"Right you are," said Grandad, "I've just made one up:

> The Man-in-the-Moon
> Came down too soon,
> He'd only done one circuit;
> He said, 'I mean, it's this machine,
> — I don't know how to work it!'"

He laughed a lot at that. Louise had noticed that Grandad often laughed a lot at his own jokes, and when he did she couldn't help laughing with him.

---

FIRST MOON MAN ON EARTH
THE EARTH MODULE HAND BOOK
EARTH MODULE
MOON
SPECIAL OCCASIONS
EARTH MAPS vol. 1
PLANTS
TO SURVIVE ON EARTH

Once again it was bed-time and Louise was having her good-night chat with her grandfather. She always enjoyed that, for he often made her giggle with the things he said, and told her stories to think over before going to sleep.

"What are you thinking about now, Grandad?" she asked.

"I can't help thinking of that pony," he said, "the one that started out as Dapple Grey. You remember,

> I lent him to a lady
> To ride a mile away,
> She whipped him and slashed him
> And rode him through the mire,
> I wouldn't lend my horse again
> For any lady's hire."

"Yes," said Louise, "that's the *old* rhyme."

"Well," said her grandfather, "although it says I wouldn't lend him again, how'd it be if we let him go back to that horrid lady? He's not so tame, now, and he might teach her a lesson."

"Oh, yes please!" cried Louise.

"Let me se now," he said.

> "I had a little pony once,
> His name was Dapple White,
> I lent him to a lady
> And he gave her quite a fright.
> He kicked and he bucked
> And he threw her on her face,
> For the way she treated ponies
> Was an absolute disgrace!"

"Lovely!" said Louise, "it served her right for being so unkind to him."

She thought over the brave little pony for a while, then feeling sleepy she slipped her arm around Grandad's neck and gave him a kiss.

"Good-night, Grandad," she said.

"Good-night, my dear," said Grandad.